TRAINS AT WORK

BOOKS BY RICHARD AMMON

The Kids' Book of Chocolate

Growing Up Amish

Trains at Work

TRAINS

BY RICHARD AMMON

AT WORK

Photographs by **Darrell Peterson and Richard Ammon**

Atheneum   1993   **New York**

Maxwell Macmillan Canada

Toronto

Maxwell Macmillan International

New York Oxford Singapore Sydney

To Cari

ACKNOWLEDGMENTS:
This book would not have been possible without the help and cooperation of many persons.

I wish to extend special thanks to James and Mary Leisey, dispatchers for Conrail, for their almost daily advice.

Also from Conrail, thanks to Marsha "Sam" Biderman, graphic services manager.

Special thanks, too, to Wendell Dillinger of the Middletown & Hummelstown Railroad, the "Milk and Honey Line," for taking the time to move the caboose into position, and to the boys and girls from the Demey Elementary School in Middletown, and their principal, Mr. Joseph Rasimas.

I also wish to thank Kathy Phillips at Northern Shipping in Philadelphia, and Satish Goel and Ronald Frey at Amstar.

And thanks to Kervin Martin of Wilbur Chocolate for his generous cooperation.

Finally, I wish to thank Marcia Marshall for her encouragement and help.

Additional photographs were supplied by Jerry Plant (title page and page 6), Douglas W. Watts (page 14), Conrail (page 13), and Ringling Bros. and Barnum & Bailey Combined Shows, Inc. (page 7).

Atheneum
Macmillan Publishing Company
866 Third Avenue
New York, NY 10022
Maxwell Macmillan Canada, Inc.
1200 Eglinton Avenue East
Suite 200
Don Mills, Ontario M3C 3N1
Macmillan Publishing Company is part of the
Maxwell Communication Group of Companies.
First edition
Printed in Singapore
10 9 8 7 6 5 4 3 2 1

Library of Congress Cataloging-in-Publication Data

Ammon, Richard.
Trains at work / by Richard Ammon; photographs by Darrell Peterson and Richard Ammon.
p. cm.
Summary : Depicts what railworkers do and how trains run and carry products, specifically chocolate products, all over the country.
ISBN 0–689–31740–9
1. Railroads—Juvenile literature. [1. Railroads.]
I. Peterson, Darrell, ill. II. Title.
TF148.A5 1993
625. 1—dc20 92–33913

The text of this book is set in 16 pt. Perpetua Bold.

Trains rush across America.

Where are they going? What are they doing?

What trains do best is move heavy loads.

The average empty car weighs about 30 tons.

But a boxcar loaded with 85 tons of cocoa beans weighs about 115 tons, while a covered hopper car loaded with about 90 tons of sugar weighs about 120 tons.

Powerful engines are needed to pull heavy cars loaded with coiled steel that will be made into anything from auto parts to toys; thousands of gallons of corn syrup; new tractors; lumber; the circus; and many people.

This is the story of how a railroad carries cocoa beans and sugar to a chocolate factory, and how the railroad helps deliver the chocolate bars to a store near you.

When a ship from Latin America docks at a big city port, men operating huge cranes unload her cargo of cocoa beans.

The bags of beans are stored in warehouses at the docks. As soon as the beans are sold to the chocolate company, a call goes out to the railroad to drop off an empty boxcar at the warehouse. A boxcar must be clean to carry cocoa beans, which will be made into chocolate.

Men driving forklift trucks move pallets piled with bags of cocoa beans from the warehouse into the railroad car. Inside the boxcar two other men stack the heavy bags.

When the car is full, the forklift pushes the heavy door shut. Then the warehouse foreman seals it by slipping a thin piece of metal through the door handle. The seal is not a lock; but just like the protective covering on a medicine bottle, this seal tells the people receiving the shipment that no one has unlawfully opened the door or tampered with the bags of cocoa beans inside.

A small engine owned by the warehouse company pulls the boxcar loaded with cocoa beans onto a siding, a short section of track that branches off the main line.

There the boxcar waits until the evening, when a big Conrail engine crawls onto the siding and couples with the boxcar to pull it to the railroad yard.

At the railroad yard, called a classification yard, cars from all over are sorted according to where they are going. To do this, each of the cars is pushed up the hump—a small hill—and then uncoupled.

As the car coasts down the other side of the hump, people in towers throw switches down in the yard, where tracks spread out like the fingers of your hands. The boxcar follows the tracks and rolls through a switch onto a siding with other cars going to the same city.

The cars on this siding become a train. When the train is made up and ready to roll, the engineer couples several engines to it.

While the engineer operates the locomotives, dispatchers control the movements of the trains. In a large room miles from any tracks, they sit before a series of monitors, overseeing a section of track fifty miles long or longer. These dispatchers watch red lines, representing trains, creep slowly along green lines of track.

Almost like someone running a model railroad, dispatchers tell trains to proceed, slow down, or stop. They even throw switches to change a train's direction.

Big blue locomotives pull cars over bridges, between hills, and through valleys to the town near the chocolate factory.

Today's locomotives produce between nine hundred and four thousand horsepower. That's from seven to thirty times more powerful than an average car. Their big diesel engines generate electricity to run the motors that turn the wheels.

To slow a train, the engineer reverses the power. This braking puts so much strain on the motors that huge fans atop the locomotives are needed to cool the engines.

To stop a train, the engineer applies the air brakes that connect each car. You can see the hoses hanging beneath the couplers. It takes the average one-hundred-car train about two miles to come to a complete stop. So, by the time an engineer sees something on the track, it's usually too late to stop in time. All he or she can do is apply the brakes and sound the horn in warning.

After traveling many miles, the boxcar of cocoa beans and several other cars are left at a track near the chocolate factory. Then the train continues its journey to the next city.

Early in the morning at the chocolate factory, the Conrail conductor of the shifter engine gets the work orders and rules for the day. The work orders tell which of the cars dropped off at the side track need to be moved and where they must go.

car of the train, the caboose carried red lights to warn trains approaching from behind.

Today you won't find cabooses at the end of long-distance trains. Instead, a red light flashes from the last car. Now cabooses only trail behind local trains that shift cars at plants and factories.

An old caboose serves as an office for the conductor and as a place to eat for the crew. In the past a caboose was a home away from home for the train crew. At night, on a long trip, the engineer would shove the caboose onto a sidetrack so the crew could sleep. In the morning they would make breakfast on the coal-burning stove before traveling on.

From a cupola on top of the caboose, or from bay windows on the sides, the flagman could keep an eye on the rear of his train. As the last

At his desk in the old caboose, the shifter conductor plans the day's work.

Trains travel on the right-hand track, just like automobiles, but the engineer sits on the right side in the engine, instead of on the left as in an automobile. That way he can see signs and signals along the side of the track.

While an engineer controls the speed of the engine, he cannot steer it. The locomotive travels only where tracks lead. To change its direction, a crew member has to turn a heavy lever that moves a small section of track.

Here, the train will go straight.

Here, the train will go to the left.

The shifter engine must travel to the siding where the boxcar of cocoa beans was set off and push it to the chocolate plant to be unloaded.

Several times a day while the shifter engine switches cars, east- or west-bound trains speed through.

The conductor calls the dispatcher for permission to cross over the main line to the siding where the boxcar and other cars are standing.

The dispatcher checks the screen and says, "Eastbound 3365 by." That means the conductor must wait and watch for an eastbound train with the number 3365.

After the eastbound passes, the shifter engine crosses over the main tracks, couples with the boxcars, and pulls them to the chocolate factory.

Long ago, switchmen standing between cars were injured when they inserted or removed pins from link-and-pin couplers.

In 1873 Eli Janney invented today's knuckle couplers. They work like hands coupled together so the thumbs hook over the knuckles.

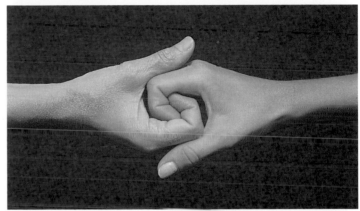

As open couplers are pushed together, a pin automatically drops into position, locking them. To uncouple cars, a crew member must pull a lever that lifts the pin and allows the coupler to open.

At the chocolate factory the yard engine spots the car, which means it pushes it to a spot where it can be unloaded.

The bags of cocoa beans are unloaded one at a time.

A workman, using hooks to grab the burlap bags, lifts the 132-pound bags of cocoa beans from the boxcar onto a conveyor belt. The belt carries the bags a short distance to where another man empties the beans into a bin. Another set of belts lifts the beans into tall silos, where they are stored.

In another city, another ship docks. This one is filled with raw sugar from the Caribbean.

After the giant shovel scoops out most of the sugar, two bulldozers are lowered into the ship's huge holds.

The bulldozers push the raw sugar into mounds for the giant shovel, which can lift tons of raw sugar in each scoopful.

The shovel dumps the sugar into a hopper that funnels it to the warehouse. An elevator lifts the raw sugar from the warehouse to the sugar plant. There, raw sugar is refined into crystals of pure sugar.

Once the sugar is refined, it is loaded into the top of a covered hopper car.

This covered hopper car is picked up by a Conrail engine and taken to the classification yard, where it becomes part of a train going to the chocolate factory.

The yard engine spots this car *inside* the chocolate factory so rats and other pests cannot get at the sugar while it is being unloaded. Hoses force air into the car. This pushes the sugar out the bottom, and then a fan blows it into a huge storage bin.

Cocoa beans, sugar, and other ingredients are combined to make chocolate!

Men driving forklifts scoot around inside the chocolate factory, loading cartons of chocolate bars into semitrailers.

The tractor-trailer trucks are driven to the piggyback rail terminal, where the trailers are loaded onto flatcars. Railroaders use the term *piggybacks* for truck trailers that ride on the backs of railroad flatcars.

A train pulls flatcars of truck trailers to your city. There the trailers are lifted off the flatcars. Trucks hook up to the trailers and deliver the candy bars to your local store.

Freight trains have carried many kinds of loads many miles to make chocolate bars, but for these kids the best part of the trip is getting to eat the chocolate.